"Compassion is the awakening of the heart
from bestial self-interest to humanity."

JOSEPH CAMPBELL

For Eric and Brian

Distributed in Canada by Douglas & McIntyre Ltd.

Color separations by Hong Kong Scanner Arts

Printed and bound in the United States by Berryville Graphics

Designed by Filomena Tuosto

First edition, 1999

Library of Congress Cataloging-in-Publication Data

Lee, Jeanne M.

I once was a monkey : stories Buddha told / Jeanne M. Lee. — 1st ed.

    p. cm.

    Summary: A retelling of six Jatakas, or birth stories, which illustrate some of the central tenets of Buddha's teachings, such as compassion, honesty, and thinking clearly before acting.

    ISBN 0-374-33548-6

    1. Tipiṭaka. Suttapiṭaka. Khuddakanikāya. Jātaka—Paraphrases, English. 2. Jataka stories, English. [1. Jataka stories.] I. Title.

    BQ1462.E5L44 1999

    294.3'82325–dc21

                                                   98-17651

JEANNE M. LEE

I Once Was a Monkey

STORIES BUDDHA TOLD

FARRAR, STRAUS AND GIROUX

NEW YORK

The monsoon came to the forest that morning. Suddenly the wind rose, ushering in dark clouds. Shrieking birds filled the treetops, and the monkey families that lived there jumped nervously from branch to branch. Then the sky exploded with thunder and streaks of lightning, and rain came pouring down. In the frenzy, a young monkey lost his footing and fell from his tree.

He scurried aimlessly on the forest floor, crying for his mother. A green snake slithered across his path, seeking cover. Frightened and whimpering, the monkey came to a clearing filled with tumbles of large rocks. Tall banyan trees encircled some of the rocks with their long roots. Between two enlarged roots, the desperate monkey found a dark cave-like opening. He ran in.

"Oof!" a creature grunted. "Who is standing on my shell?"

The little monkey jumped aside as what he thought was a rock began to move.

"Ouch! My paw!" barked another animal.

"Watch where you are going, stranger!" a third animal roared.

Several eyes were upon him in the dark. Everywhere he turned, it seemed he was facing an animal larger than himself. The small monkey squealed in terror.

"Up here, little one," called a gentle voice. "I have space for you."

He looked up and saw two tiny eyes. Quickly he climbed a jumble of stones to where a white dove was perched.

"Thank you," the monkey said shyly.

As his eyes became accustomed to the gloomy light, the monkey saw the big turtle whose back he had stood on, the jackal whose paw he had stepped on, and the fierce lion he had almost bumped into. It was stifling in the small enclosure.

"Just one more body to heat up this miserable place," growled the jackal.

"Let's turn him out," said the turtle.

"No, there's space for him," said the dove.

The lion gave a loud roar. "Can we have quiet in here!" he demanded.

"Quiet, yourself," barked the jackal.

"Why, you ugly—"

"Hush, children, hush," came a whisper.

The startled animals turned their heads toward the voice. There, in a deep recess at the far corner of the cave, a stone statue sat in front of a glowing halo, his face tranquil and his hands raised as if showing the way.

"Hush, children," the statue said again. "The monsoon rains in this part of the forest sometimes last many days. Listen, I will tell you a story to pass the time."

The monkey sighed with relief, glad to be left alone.

THE FOOLISH FOREST SPRITE

Long long ago, said the statue, I was born a sprite in a young forest. My friend, another forest sprite, ruled in a large adjacent forest, home to all kinds of wild animals.

Now, at the time, a mighty lion lived in my friend's forest with his family, hunting and feeding on the smaller animals. Too often, the lions killed more than they could eat, and the abandoned carcasses of their prey rotted in the sun, creating a foul smell throughout the land. My friend was very distressed by this disorderly state of affairs.

One day, he told me he had decided to chase the lions out of his forest. I advised him that it was an unwise thing to do.

"The lions protect your beautiful forest," I said to him. "When they are gone, farmers from the nearby villages will come without fear to cut down your trees and cultivate your land. Soon your forest will be gone. The other animals, and you, too, will have to find a new home. Please think again."

Alas, my friend did not listen. He took the form of a horrifying ogre one morning and drove away the lion and his family.

As I had predicted, the villagers soon noted the absence of lion tracks. They started cutting down his trees and clearing the land. My friend went to the lions and begged them to return, but they refused.

The lions took refuge in my forest. The other wild animals soon followed. And my foolish friend? He roamed the earth looking for another home.

 "I remember how sad I felt about the destruction of the forest," said the statue. "I wished I had been able to convince my friend that all creatures depend on one another for their existence. Only tolerance of others will bring harmony."

The animals in the cave were silent. Outside, the heavy monsoon rains continued.

"Who are you who are so wise?" the white dove asked.

"I am Gautama Buddha, the Enlightened One," the statue replied. "The piles of stones outside used to be my temple. But the men who built it quarreled, and during their wars my temple was destroyed, except for this small sanctuary now hidden by the roots of the trees."

"Stories are well and good, but I am hungry!" growled the lion.

"There was someone who was very hungry in one of my past lives," said the Buddha. "Listen to this story."

THE DECEITFUL HERON

I was then a willow tree on a hill. On one side of the hill was a small pond; on the other side, a large, clear lake. It was toward the end of summer, and it had not rained for many weeks. The pond was drying up. The many fish and the one red crab that lived there were crowding one another as they swam in the muddy water.

One stiflingly hot day, a black heron flew by. He noticed the many fish in the shallow pond. How he wished to eat them all! He went and stood on one leg in the middle of the water.

Curious, the fish approached. "What are you doing in our midst, Heron? Are you thinking of making a meal of us?"

"No, I just feel sorry for all of you in this warm muddy puddle when you could be living in the large cool lake over there," said the heron, gesturing with his beak in the direction of the hill.

"But how can we know if a lake truly lies beyond that hill?" asked the skeptical fish.

"I could take one of you to scout the lake first. Then he can come back and tell you all about it," the heron suggested.

A tough old fish volunteered to go with him. The heron picked up the old fish with his beak, flew over the hill, and let him drop into the cool water of the lake. The old fish swam under the lotus flowers and scouted around the edges of the lake. The bird told the truth! The old fish saw the abundance of food and he was satisfied. The heron took him back to the muddy pond to report the good news.

After hearing the old fish's description, the whole school decided to move to the lake, just as the heron had expected. The old fish was the first to go. The crafty heron picked him up with his beak and flew over the hill, but instead of putting him in the lake, he flew straight to me. He dropped the wriggling fish in a notch between two of my branches, and he tore the flesh off the poor creature until only bones were left.

One at a time, the unsuspecting fish from the small pond were carried

to me and devoured by the heron. The foot of my trunk gradually disappeared under a heap of bones. Now only the crab was left.

"It's your turn to move to the lake," the heron said to the red crab. "Let me pick you up with my beak."

The red crab was suspicious. He devised a plan to protect himself.

"I am all ready to move, Heron," he replied. "But my hard shell will hurt your tongue. Let me hold on to your neck with my claws."

"All right, then. Let's go," said the heron.

Again, the greedy bird flew straight to my branches.

"Why are we here?" cried the red crab.

"I'm going to eat you up," chortled the bird. "Just like the others!"

"Not so fast," said the crab, tightening his grip on the heron's neck. "Take me to the lake right now, or I will snap your neck!"

"Loosen your claws!" shrieked the heron. "I will fly you there!"

As soon as they had landed at the lake's edge, the crab squeezed his claws hard on the heron's neck, killing the villain. Then slowly he made his way into the cool water, weeping all the while for his lost friends.

"I witnessed this awful thing with pain, but being a tree, I was held down by my roots and could move only with the wind. I swore that I would strive to be born as an animal in my next life so that I could help defend weak creatures against deceitful ones."

There was silence in the cave, except for the sniffling of the dove, who was crying softly.

"It was wrong of the heron to have tricked the fish," said the lion. "I would not have acted dishonestly, even if I was hungry. He deserved his fate."

"In life," said the Buddha, "there is no reward for untruthfulness. If you trick others and are cruel to them, they will behave the same way toward you in the end."

"The poor fish," said the turtle with a sigh. "I understand why they wanted to move. I would like to be in that cool lake right now."

"At one time, I too wanted to move to a better place," said the Buddha. "That was when I was born a monkey. Let me tell you what happened."

The small monkey strained his ears to listen.

THE MONKEY AND THE CROCODILE

I once was a monkey, strong and nimble, living in a forest near the Ganges River. Now and then, I would go to the river to drink. The Ganges was full of crocodiles and I was careful where I stepped, because the crafty creatures often lay hidden on the muddy banks.

One day, I spotted a huge crocodile near one of my drinking spots.

"Come closer, Monkey, don't be afraid," he called to me. "Have a drink of water, I want to tell you something."

When he saw that I wasn't going to move closer, he said to me, "I notice you here often. Do you ever leave this side of the river?"

"No," I said. "I am happy here."

"Do you know that there are more fruit trees on the other side? Trees whose branches are heavy with ripe mangoes, rose apples, and jackfruit?"

My mouth was watering as I listened to him name those delicious fruits. "I cannot cross this wide river," I said. "I do not swim."

"Climb on my back," said the crocodile. "I will take you across."

Without thinking, I jumped on his back. When we were in the middle of the river, the crocodile began to lower himself into the water.

"What are you doing?" I screamed. "You are drowning me!"

"That's exactly what I'm doing! I am going to eat your heart!"

"Why didn't you tell me before?" I said, trying to sound calm. "I could have saved you the trouble. We monkeys never bring our hearts with us when we go near the water."

"Where do you leave them, then?" asked the crocodile, very annoyed.

"We always leave them hanging on our fig tree," I said, pointing to a fig tree on the riverbank. "See that big red shape there, that's my heart. I will take it down for you if you bring me back."

The crocodile turned around. As soon as we reached land, I jumped off his back and scampered up the tree.

"Tricky Crocodile! You thought you could fool me!" I cried. "You can't even tell a fig from a monkey's heart!"

The foolish old creature was so embarrassed he dropped to the depths of the river without a sound.

The animals in the cave all laughed.

"Monkey almost lost his heart!" exclaimed the dove. "Little Monkey, aren't you glad to be here with us, rather than on the back of that crocodile?"

The monkey smiled.

"Are you feeling better now?" the Buddha asked him.

"Yes, thank you," said the monkey shyly.

"Wise Buddha, should we never believe what people tell us?" asked the jackal. "You were nearly eaten by the crocodile when you believed him."

"Well, my smart friend," replied the Buddha, "I was greedy for the delicious fruit; therefore, I was ready to believe the crocodile without thinking. It is best always to keep a clear mind, to think before we act. I have another story to illustrate this."

THE FLIGHT OF THE BEASTS

I was a lion living in a forest near the ocean. In this forest, at the foot of an old mango tree, a young hare lived in a hole, protected by the wide canopy of tree branches. This little hare was a worrywart.

One day, as he lay resting in the dark, the hare had a frightening thought: What will happen to me if the good earth suddenly caves in?

Just then a huge ripe mango fell to the ground with a crash, right above the little hare's hole.

The earth is indeed caving in! thought the hare. He shot out of his hole and ran off in a panic.

His cousin, who saw his frightened look, called to him, "What is the matter? Why are you running off in such a state?" The timid hare yelled back without stopping, "The earth is caving in! I am running away." His cousin immediately joined him. Another hare saw the commotion, and joined them; soon another did the same, until the whole family of hares was racing through the forest. A deer in a bamboo grove saw the flight of hares and asked a straggler the reason. "The earth is caving in! The world is coming to an end!" the creature squeaked. Without hesitating, the deer joined them in their panicky flight; and soon all his relatives had joined as well. Then came the wild boars, the oxen, the rhinoceros, the tigers, and even the elephants.

As the stampeding animals passed my lair, I heard their cries that the earth was caving in. But I did not hear the rumbling of an earthquake, and the world did not show any sign of coming to an end. I decided I had to stop them, for they were racing toward the ocean and would all drown.

I caught up with the leaders just as they reached the beach. I gave my roar three times to stop their flight.

"Who saw the earth caving in?" I asked. "Did you see it, Elephants?"

"We didn't," said the elephants, "but the tigers did."

"We didn't," said the tigers. "The rhinoceros did."

"We didn't," said the rhinoceros. "The oxen did."

"We didn't," said the oxen. "The wild boars did."

"We didn't," said the wild boars. "The deer did."

"We didn't," said the deer. "The hares did."

"None of us saw it," the hares said, "except for our little cousin."

"I didn't see it," the timid young hare said. "But I heard it as I was resting and thinking what would happen if the good earth came to an end."

"Where were you resting, little one?" I asked.

"In my hole, at the foot of an old mango tree," he said.

I knew then what probably had caused the sound. I addressed the animals: "Wait here. I will go and find out what happened. Little Hare, show me the way to your hole."

I put the frightened creature on my back and ran to his home. As he had described, his hole was at the foot of an ancient mango tree, and as I suspected, a big ripe mango was lying next to it.

"The noise you heard was from the fall of this fruit," I said to the hare. "That's all."

We went back to the beach and told the others what had occurred.

 "Silly hare," said the turtle. "But he's not the only one who's afraid of big noise. I was terrified of the thunder earlier, before I found this cave."

"Now I understand why we shouldn't believe everything we hear," said the jackal. "I hope I would be as prudent as the lion in the story."

"He was also brave," roared the lion proudly. He seemed to have forgotten his hunger for the moment.

"Wise Buddha, have you ever been a dove in your past lives?" asked the white dove.

"In fact, I was one," answered the Buddha.

THE WISE DOVE

I was once a gray dove living in a wood near a palace. One day, I was pecking for loose seeds with my cousins when suddenly a net fell on us. As we struggled to free ourselves, a fat man stooped and gathered the net with us in it.

"Ha, ha, ha!" he laughed. "Here is a fine feast for the King."

He took us to the palace kitchens and put us in a bamboo cage. We were trapped.

Morning and night, the man, who was the palace cook, put grain and water in our cage. I thought and thought. If I ate and grew fatter, I would be killed and fed to the King; but if I shrank to skin and bones, I might be spared. So I decided to abstain from the food.

My famished cousins ate everything. They would not listen to my reasoning; they thought I was mad not to partake of the feast. Every time I was tempted to peck at the grain, I would take a sip of water instead.

Many days went by. Then one night the cook came to the cage and looked in. "Time for a taste!" he muttered gleefully. His plump hand reached in the cage and snatched a cousin away. My other cousins were now terrified.

Early the next day, the cook appeared again. One by one, he took all my cousins away. Then he came to me. "What happened to you?" he exclaimed. "You must be sick; it's not even worth my while to wring your neck. Go away!"

I flew out of the cage and escaped through a window.

 "Thank you for the story, Wise Teacher," said the dove. "I wonder whether I would have had the gray dove's endurance if I was caught."

"Endurance can be achieved through practice," said the Buddha. "And because of it, the gray dove lived."

"Buddha," said the jackal, "there are no jackals in your stories."

"I have been a jackal at one time or another," said the Buddha. "But you know, my friend, our actions are much more important than what we are, because our actions determine what we will be in our next life. We might be something other than what we are today. You are a jackal now, but you might be a lion or something else in your next life.

"This story that I am going to tell you before the rain ends also shows how our actions can affect our friends.

"Listen."

THREE FRIENDS IN A FOREST

Long ago, I was born a golden antelope in a thick forest. Often I would go and drink at a lake near my home. There I met a green turtle and we became good friends. Not long after, a woodpecker made his nest in a tree on the bank of the lake; he, too, became our friend. So whenever I went down to the lake, the three of us would talk, enjoying one another's company.

One autumn day, there was a beautiful sunset. I thought how enjoyable it would be to share the moment with my two friends. I was happily running toward the lake when I heard a loud snap. I screeched in pain as a snare tightened around my leg. I had stepped on a trap set by a hunter who lived nearby.

Woodpecker was beside me right away, offering comfort and advice. Then Turtle appeared, and he said, "Try to keep calm, Antelope. The more you move, the tighter the hunter's snare will be. We will find a way to get you out."

It was decided that Turtle would gnaw through the thick leather strap of the snare while Woodpecker would do his best to keep the hunter away, for surely he must have heard my cry for help.

Turtle started immediately with his tedious task, while Woodpecker flew to the hunter's lodge.

The hunter had indeed heard my cry. As Woodpecker arrived, he was stepping out his front door, a sharp knife in his hand. Woodpecker didn't waste any time but flew straight into the man's face, again and again. Disoriented, the hunter staggered back into his house. Woodpecker thought: The man will try his rear door now. I will wait for him there.

The hunter was opening his back door just as Woodpecker arrived. Again the brave bird flew into the man's face, and this time he succeeded in pecking one of his eyes. The man cried out in pain and retreated into his house, slamming the door. Woodpecker kept watch, but the hunter stayed inside, probably to nurse his eye.

A few hours later, he appeared at his front door with the sharp knife in his hand. But now he was wearing a wide-brimmed hat to protect his face. Woodpecker flew quickly to his friends.

"The hunter is coming! The hunter is coming!" Woodpecker warned. Through the trees, I saw silver flashes of sunlight glinting from the hunter's knife. Turtle had chewed through most of the strap of the snare. Gathering all my strength, I gave a great yank and broke loose. I ran off, but from the safety of the trees I saw that my friend Turtle was caught. The hunter was angry when he saw his broken snare; he threw Turtle in a sack and hung it on the branch of a tree. Then he looked around for me.

I knew I had to help my friend Turtle, who had just saved me. I let myself be seen by the hunter, pretending to be hurt. I led him to another

part of the forest, then I ran back to the lake. Woodpecker was already there, fluttering around the sack where Turtle was held. I lifted it with my antlers, and the sack came tumbling to the ground. We loosened the opening so Turtle could crawl out.

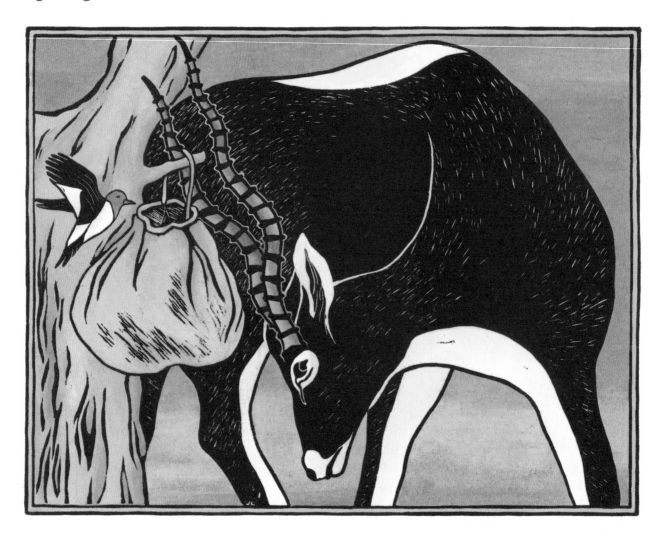

Then I said to my friends, "Thank you both for saving my life. But we have to say goodbye for a little while. I will go back to the thickest part of the forest; you, Woodpecker, will have to move your nest; and you, my dear Turtle, please go back to the deepest part of the lake. The angry hunter will soon forget this whole thing and then we can be together again." And so we bade each other farewell.

 "And now, my children," said the Buddha, "we have come to the end of my last story. The rain will stop soon and it is time to say goodbye. Remember my words: Be truthful, be kind to one another, and you will attain peace. We will meet again in another life."

Sometime later, the small monkey rubbed his eyes. He seemed to have fallen asleep, but for how long, he didn't know. He looked around the sanctuary. Bright light was seeping through the cracks between the stones.

"Good morning, Monkey," the white dove greeted, stretching his wings and his short legs. He cried, "Wake up, everybody! The rain has stopped! Wake up!"

There was stirring in the cave as the other animals awoke.

"Good morning, everyone," said the small monkey.

"Good morning, Monkey," grunted the jackal, standing up. "Good morning, Dove; good morning, Turtle; and good morning to you, Lion."

"What a long nap!" said the turtle. "I can't wait to go back to the lake."

"And I am ready for a meal!" exclaimed the lion. He yawned loudly. "I want to say goodbye to the Buddha first. Wise Buddha, we are leaving now, thank you for telling us all those stories. Wise Buddha?"

There was no answer. The animals all turned toward the far corner; the battered stone statue of Buddha in the recess was silent. There was no halo behind him, but the face of the statue still had his tranquil smile, and his hands were raised as if he was teaching.

"But the stories . . . Didn't the Buddha tell us stories?" the animals asked one another. They all remembered them, but the Buddha did not respond. The animals spoke to the statue a few more times, then finally bade each other a polite goodbye. The lion left first, followed by the white dove. As they were waiting for the turtle to crawl out of the cave, the jackal said to the young monkey, "If you jump on my back, friend, I could give you a ride home."

"Thank you, Jackal," the monkey replied. "But after sleeping for so long, I'd like to stretch and run a bit. I am sure we will meet again in this forest."

"Goodbye, then," said the jackal. "Goodbye, Turtle!"

"Goodbye, Jackal," said the turtle. "Goodbye, Monkey. Come visit me when you go to drink at the lake."

"Farewell, Turtle," said the monkey. He was the last animal to step out into the sun.

Two ants scuttled near his foot, carrying bits of leaves. He raised his foot to step on them as he had always enjoyed doing. Then he stopped himself. He suddenly remembered the Buddha's words. But it was hard to believe the stone statue had spoken.

"Was it just a dream, then?" he asked, scratching his head.

AFTERWORD

The six stories retold in this book are called Jatakas, or birth stories, in Buddhist literature. Siddhartha Gautama Buddha, who was born 2,500 years ago, told the Jatakas to his disciples on special occasions, to illustrate his teachings. He was born a wealthy and happy prince, but once he saw how sickness, old age, and death caused misery outside his palace walls, he resolved to find a way to overcome human suffering. He abandoned his rich and pampered life, and after a long and arduous period of meditation, he found a spiritual answer to his quest. Buddha became a famous teacher, and he established an order of monks to continue his work.

For the curious, OLD PATH WHITE CLOUDS by Thich Nhat Hanh recounts the life of Siddhartha Gautama Buddha from when he left his palace and became a hermit, through his enlightenment, his preaching life, and his death, all in the words of one of his young disciples. "The Deceitful Heron" and "Three Friends in a Forest" are retold in Thich Nhat Hanh's book. For a complete collection of the Jatakas, which number over five hundred in all, read THE JATAKA OR STORIES OF THE BUDDHA'S FORMER BIRTHS, edited by E. B. Cowell.

Lee, Jeanne M.

I once was a monkey.

DATE		

BAKER & TAYLOR